Mr. Munday
and the Space Creatures

By Bonnie Pryor • Illustrated by Lee Lorenz

Simon & Schuster Books for Young Readers
Published by Simon & Schuster
New York · London · Toronto · Sydney · Tokyo · Singapore

SIMON & SCHUSTER BOOKS FOR YOUNG READERS
Simon & Schuster Building, Rockefeller Center, 1230 Avenue of the Americas, New York, New York 10020.
Text copyright © 1989 by Bonnie Pryor. Illustrations copyright © 1989 by Lee Lorenz.
SIMON & SCHUSTER BOOKS FOR YOUNG READERS is a trademark of Simon & Schuster.
Manufactured in the United States of America

10 9 8 7 6 5 4 3 2 1   (pbk.) 10 9 8 7 6 5 4 3 2 1

Library of Congress Cataloging in Publication Data:
Pryor, Bonnie. Mr. Munday and the space creatures.
Summary: When bumbling mailman Mr. Munday trades places with a space creature,
everyone gets unexpectedly wonderful surprises.
[1. Postal service—Letter Carriers—Fiction.   2. Science fiction.]
I. Lorenz, Lee, ill.   II. Title. PZ7.P94965Mq   1989
ISBN 0-671-67114-6   88-19798   ISBN: 0-671-73620-5 (pbk.)

"What a boring night," said Mr. Munday to his fat cat,
Harry. "I wish something exciting would happen."

Just then there was a knock on the door. "Hello," said a something-or-other when Mr. Munday opened the door. "My name is Fingle, and this is my pet, Dink. I always wanted to meet an earth man."

"Come in," said Mr. Munday. "My name is Mr. Munday, and this is my cat, Harry. I'm very glad to meet you."

"*Meowww,*" screeched Harry. His hair stuck straight out.

"*Orge, orge,*" said Dink.

Fingle came in and sat down on Mr. Munday's favorite chair. "Would you like some tea?" asked Mr. Munday politely.

"What is that?" asked the space creature.

Mr. Munday made two cups of tea. He poured a bowl of milk for Dink and Harry.

Fingle stuck his thumb in the tea. "Delicious," he said.

"Why did you come to Earth?" Mr. Munday asked.

"My spaceship broke down. I decided to take a walk while it was being fixed." Fingle sighed and continued.

"Space is very boring. There is nothing to look at but stars and planets, stars and planets."

"It sounds exciting to me," said Mr. Munday. "All I ever do is deliver the mail."

"That sounds like fun," said Fingle. "Would you like to change places for a while?"

"I don't think my uniform would fit you," said Mr. Munday. "You have too many arms."

"I could hide two of them," said Fingle.

"Amazing," said Mr. Munday. "But what should I wear?"

"Whatever you like," said Fingle. "I'll call the captain and tell him you're coming."

Mr. Munday grabbed his cap, put a sandwich and some clean socks in his lunchbox, and ran off to the spaceship.

"It's about time," said the captain. "We're just about to blast off."

All the space creatures sat down in the spaceship. Mr. Munday sat down, too.

"Don't forget to push the red button," said the captain.

"Do you mean this one?" asked Mr. Munday. He tapped the button. All of a sudden the rocket took off with a terrible *whoosh*.

"Great galloping spacemen," yelled the captain. "You pushed the button too soon. Now we will land on the planet Grogg."

"Is that bad?" asked Mr. Munday.

"You'll find out," said the space creatures.

Mr. Munday looked out the window. He could see stars and planets, stars and planets. It was very exciting. But he was a little worried about the planet Grogg.

Meanwhile back on Earth, Fingle was getting ready for his first day of work.

"I wonder where earth people keep all their food?" said Fingle.

Then he found a cupboard full of cans and boxes. "Earth people keep strange things inside their cans," he said to Dink. "But these boxes are delicious."

Fingle wanted to look just like a real mailman. He polished his buttons and shined his shoes.

He tucked two of his arms inside Mr. Munday's coat and pulled his hat down over his extra eye. He looked very handsome in an unearthly sort of way.

Fingle started down the street with a bag full of letters.
But when he stepped on a strange contraption with
wheels, it started to roll down the hill.

"Stop," yelled Fingle. But the thing only rolled faster.

Finally it crashed into a tree and Fingle landed right in the middle of Mrs. Grumbles's flower bed.

"You are smashing my petunias," shouted Mrs. Grumbles. She chased Fingle down the street with a hoe. "Sorry, madam," said Fingle. "It won't happen again."

Later on, a little boy started yelling at him.
"That's the man who stole my skateboard," cried the boy.

"Shame on you," said his mother. She hit Fingle over
the head with her umbrella.

The next day three big dogs chased Fingle up a tree.

"I never knew being a mailman was so hard," Fingle said with a sigh. He sat in Mr. Munday's favorite chair and took off his shoes. Every one of his fourteen toes had a blister.

Just then the telephone rang. Dink did not like the strange sound. He jumped up and knocked the telephone off the table.

"This is the radio station," said a voice. "Washington was the first president of the United States. If you can tell me his first name, you will win ten million dollars."

"*Orge, orge,*" said Dink.

"That's right," said the man. "George Washington. We will deliver your prize tomorrow."

The next day three big trucks came to Mr. Munday's house. Some men carried in sacks of money. *"Orge, orge,"* cried Dink. Mr. Munday's whole house was filled with sacks of money.

When Fingle came home from delivering the mail, he could not believe his eyes. "Look at all these green letters. How will I know where they go? I guess I will just have to give some to everyone."

While Fingle was sorting all the green mail, Mr. Munday had just landed on the planet Grogg. Five hundred Grogg creatures slithered out to meet him.

"We love company," said the Groggians. "You must come to a feast."

"I don't know why I was worried. The Groggians seem very nice," said Mr. Munday.

"*Meoww*," cried Harry. He jumped right into Mr. Munday's arms.

"They only eat broccoli," said the space creatures.
"Broccoli soup, baked broccoli, fried broccoli. And for
dessert, broccoli pie. We hate broccoli."

"I *love* broccoli," said Mr. Munday.

"Hooray," said the Groggians. "We will make you our
king. You can stay with us forever."

"*Meow*," said Harry. He didn't like broccoli one bit. He
also did not like the Grogg creatures.

The Groggians gave Mr. Munday a crown. They made him sit on a throne shaped like a giant broccoli.

"We warned you," said the space creatures. "Now they will never let you go."

Mr. Munday had an idea. "I like my broccoli with cheese," he told the Groggians.

"What is cheese?" asked the Grogg creatures.

"It is round and yellow," said Mr. Munday. "I am the king. You must find me some cheese."

The Groggians were very upset. They did not want the king to be unhappy. They looked everywhere for some cheese.

As soon as they were gone, Mr. Munday got off his throne. The second he did, a giant alarm started to ring.

"Run," cried the space creatures. All the Groggians came slithering back.

Mr. Munday picked up Harry. He ran all the way back to the spaceship. The Groggians were right behind.

"Come back," cried the Groggians. "We love you."

The space creatures slammed the door just in time.
"Where would you like to go now?" they asked.

"Home," said Mr. Munday. "Space is very interesting.
But I miss my own little house."
"*Meow,*" said Harry.

"I am sorry," said Fingle when Mr. Munday got home. "I didn't get all the mail delivered. There are still five sacks of these strange green letters."

"I'll take care of the rest of these," said Mr. Munday. "That's very kind of you," said Fingle.

"I hope you didn't get too bored," said Mr. Munday.
"Oh no," said Fingle. "Being a mailman is too exciting
for me. I will be glad to get back to stars and planets."

"I will be glad to get back to delivering mail," said Mr.
Munday. "But come back anytime."

"Goodbye," said Fingle. He waved all four of his arms.

"*Orge, orge,*" said Dink.

Mr. Munday sat down in his favorite chair, and Harry jumped up in his lap. They both closed their eyes. "It's good to be home," said Mr. Munday.

Harry opened one eye. "*Meow*," he purred.